This Walker book belongs to:

_____

_____

_____

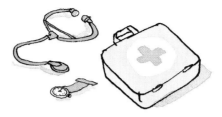

Simon James is an award-winning author and illustrator of books for children
and is a regular speaker in schools and at festivals across the UK and the US.
His books include *George Flies South*, *Dear Greenpeace*, *Sally and the Limpet*,
Leon and Bob, *The Day Jake Vacuumed* and the bestselling Baby Brains series.
Simon likes to draw with a dip pen and uses watercolour paints
for his illustrations. To find out more about Simon James
and his books, visit www.simonjamesbooks.com

First published 2013 by Walker Books Ltd
87 Vauxhall Walk, London SE11 5HJ

2 4 6 8 10 9 7 5 3 1

© 2013 Simon James

This book has been typeset in Goudy
Printed in China

British Library Cataloguing in Publication Data:
a catalogue record for this book is available from the British Library

ISBN 978-1-4063-3862-1

www.walker.co.uk

Simon James

Nurse Clementine

WALKER BOOKS

AND SUBSIDIARIES

LONDON · BOSTON · SYDNEY · AUCKLAND

It was Clementine Brown's birthday.
Mr and Mrs Brown bought her
a nurse's outfit and a first aid kit.

"It's just what I wanted," she said.

"You can call me 'Nurse Clementine' from now on!"

Nurse Clementine didn't have to wait long for her first emergency.

Mr Brown banged his toe on the living room door.

Straight away Nurse Clementine got to work.

"You'll need to keep this on for a week," she said.

"A week?" moaned Mr Brown.

"A week," said Nurse Clementine firmly.

Next, Mrs Brown complained she had a headache. Nurse Clementine gave her a complete check-up.

Her ears were okay, her tongue wasn't spotty and her temperature was normal.

So, just to be safe, Nurse Clementine bandaged
her head.
"You'll have to keep this on for a week," she said.
"A week?" sighed Mrs Brown.
"A week," said Nurse Clementine firmly.

In the kitchen,
Nurse Clementine
found Wellington
licking his paw.

It must be sore, decided
Nurse Clementine.
She bandaged it up
as best she could.

Nurse Clementine was very pleased with her
work. She rushed off to find her brother Tommy.
He was bound to need some help.

Bold and fearless, Tommy the superhero
was on his way down the stairs.

"Look out, Tommy!" shouted Clementine.
"You're going to hit—

the door!" Nurse Clementine immediately opened her first aid kit. "It's a good job I'm here," she said.

"No, it's not!" said Tommy. "I don't need a nurse."

"I'm Super Tommy, watch me fly.
I can leap from sofas."

"Oh, look out, Tommy!"
said Clementine.
"You're going to hit—

the floor!"
"Ouch!" said Tommy.

Nurse Clementine rushed over with her stethoscope.
She told Tommy to keep still while she checked
him for breaks and bruises.

"I'm not broken," said
Tommy. "And I told
you before, I *don't*
need a nurse.
Leave me alone!"

Tommy marched
off towards the
garden.

Clementine sat while Tommy played.

There was no one left to take care of.

She would just have to practise nursing by herself.
First, she listened for her own heartbeat.

Then, she practised bandaging on the drainpipe.

But it was no good.
"Nurses need someone to look after," Clementine sighed.

Then, she heard a voice calling
from up in the tree.
"Clementine! Clementine!
It's me," said Tommy.

"I'm stuck!" he cried. "I can't get down –
it's too high!"

"Hang on, Tommy!"
called Clementine,
"I'll get you down."

Clementine knew
she had to think
quickly.

After all, this was
a **real** emergency.

Clementine was on tiptoe but she couldn't reach Tommy.

"I'm slipping," he said.

"Hold on," said Nurse Clementine.

"I can't!" said Tommy. "I'm going to fall."

Tommy closed his eyes as his hands slipped.

But Nurse Clementine was there to catch him.

"I've got you," she said.

Tommy was relieved to be back on the ground. "Thanks, Clementine," he said, "you were great!"

When Tommy turned to go, Clementine noticed something. "Tommy," she said. "You've grazed your arm!" "Have I?" said Tommy.

"You can bandage
it if you like."

Nurse Clementine
was delighted to help.
This was going to be
her best bandage yet.
But there was one
small problem …

she had forgotten her scissors!

"This is going to be an extra
special superhero bandage,"
said Nurse Clementine.
"Really?" said Tommy.
"But you're going to
have to keep it on
all week," said
Clementine, firmly.

"All week?" said Tommy. "Great!"

The End

Stethoscope

Watch

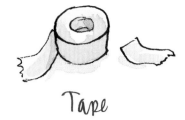

Tape

Eye Patch

Chocolate

Blood Pressure Monitor

Case

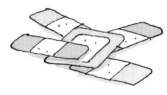

Plasters

Bandages

Otoscope

Name Badge

Reflex Hammer

Spatula

More bandages

Hat

Thermometer

Gloves

Cotton wool

Pen light

Emergency Toffees

Scissors

Tweezers

First Aid Book

Wipes